RYAN
THE LION

BRIAN OGDEN

ILLUSTRATED BY LYNNE FARMER

Scripture Union

These stories also appear in *Aunt Emily's African Animals*, a resource book of stories and activity ideas for teachers of infants.

By the same author
Maximus Mouse
Maximus Rides again
Maximus and the Great Expedition
Short tails and Tall Stories
Maximus and the Computer Mouse
Tales of Young Maximus

Maximus and the lettuce thieves
Maximus and the television
Maximus goes on holiday
Maximus has a bad day

Aunt Emily's African Animals

© Brian Ogden 1999
First published 1999

Scripture Union, 207–209 Queensway, Bletchley, Milton Keynes, MK2 2EB, England.

ISBN 1 85999 318 4

British Library Cataloguing-in-Publication Data.
A catalogue record of this book is available from the British Library.

Cover design by Ian Butterworth.
Illustrations by Lynne Farmer.

Printed and bound in Great Britain by Creative Print and Design (Wales), Ebbw Vale.

CONTENTS

INTRODUCTION

The stories in *Ryan the Lion* are told by Aunt Emily. Aunt Emily lives in a beautiful part of the world – East Africa. Most days, when she has finished cooking or cleaning, Aunt Emily likes to sit down. She sits outside in the shade. As soon as the children see her they come over.

"Tell us a story, please, Aunt Emily," say the children.

"I will when you are sitting down," says Aunt Emily.

All Aunt Emily's stories are about animals that live in East Africa. There's Ryan the lion, Sid the kid, Jock the croc and lots more. Somehow the animals seem to have the same sort of adventures that you and I have.

At the end of each story there is a prayer. This is because God loves us and cares about everything we do.

So let's join the children and sit and hear Aunt Emily telling US a story.

Brian Ogden

Chapter one

RYAN THE LION

Aunt Emily was sitting in her chair.

She had just had her tea.

The children saw Aunt Emily in her chair.

The children ran to Aunt Emily.

"Tell us a story, please," they said.

"I will when you are sitting down," said Aunt Emily.

"I will tell you a story about a lion.

The name of the lion was Ryan.

Ryan the lion was not always a good lion.

Ryan was a big and strong lion.

Ryan had a very loud roar.

When Ryan roared, the trees shook.

When Ryan roared, the birds flew off.

When Ryan roared, small animals ran away and hid.

When Ryan roared, big animals put their paws over their ears.

Ryan liked to roar.

It made him feel big.

It made him feel stronger than all the other animals.

Ryan roared more and more and more and more.

Ryan roared when he woke up in the morning.

Ryan roared before he had his lunch.

Ryan roared before he went to sleep.

Sometimes he even roared in his dreams.

Ryan roared at Brenda the zebra.

Ryan roared at James the elephant.

Ryan even roared at Kate the snake.

One day Ryan woke up and tried to roar.

But no roar came out.

Ryan tried again, but still no roar came.

Ryan could not roar because his throat was sore.

Lions cannot roar with sore throats.

The other animals were glad.

Brenda the zebra was glad.

James the elephant was glad.

And even Kate the snake was glad.

The jungle was quiet without Ryan's roars.

The trees did not shake.

The birds did not fly away.

The small animals did not hide.

The large animals did not put their paws over their ears.

All the animals went to see Ryan.

'Ryan,' they said, 'we like you but we don't like your roar.

Please don't roar any more.'

Ryan sat and thought.

'I'm sorry,' said Ryan, 'I didn't think about you.

I only thought about me.

I won't roar any more.'

All the animals were glad when they heard this.

And the sun smiled on Ryan and all the other animals."

"Thank you, Aunt Emily," said the children.

"That was a good story."

Loving Father,
it is easy to think of ourselves.
Help us to think about other people
and how we can be kind to them.
Amen.

Chapter two

BRENDA THE ZEBRA

One day Aunt Emily looked into her mirror.

"My hair is going grey," she said.

She sat down on her chair.

The children saw Aunt Emily and ran to her.

"Tell us a story, please," they said.

"I will when you are sitting down," said Aunt Emily.

"I will tell you a story about a zebra.

The name of the zebra was Brenda.

Zebras are not always clever animals.

One day Brenda the zebra was having a drink from the pool.

After she had had her drink she saw herself in the pool.

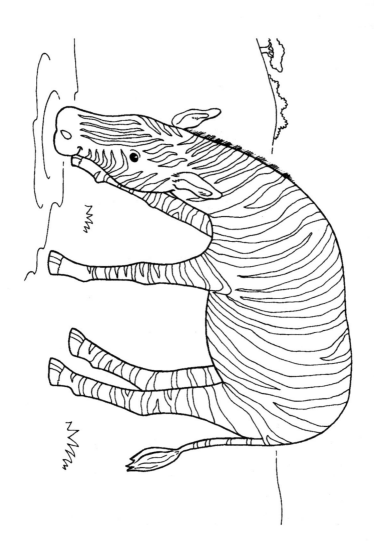

'Oh, dear,' said Brenda, 'I have some grey stripes.

I don't like having grey stripes.

I must do something about it.'

Brenda went to see James the elephant.

James did not know what to do.

Brenda went to see Ryan the lion.

Ryan did not know what to do.

Brenda even went to see Kate the snake.

Kate *did* know what to do.

'What you need is some paint,' said Kate the snake.

'If you get some black paint you can paint over your grey stripes.'

'Thank you,' said Brenda. 'You are a clever snake, Kate.'

Brenda got some black paint and she got a paint brush.

'But I can't paint myself!' she said. 'I need some help.'

'I will help you,' said James the elephant.

James took the paintbrush in his trunk.

He put the brush into the paint.

'Stand very still, Brenda,' said James.

James slowly painted over all Brenda the zebra's stripes.

He started near Brenda's face and ended
with Brenda's tail.

'Now you are black all over,' said James.

'Thank you, James,' said Brenda, 'thank
you very much.'

Brenda went to the pool.

She looked at the water.

She was black all over – all the grey stripes
had gone.

'That's better,' said Brenda. 'Now I don't
look grey.'

Brenda showed Ryan the lion.

Brenda even showed Kate the snake.

'Thank you, Kate,' said Brenda.

'That was a good idea of yours.'

At that moment the sun hid behind a big black cloud.

Soon rain began to fall from the big black cloud.

The rain began to fall on Brenda the zebra.

The rain fell on the black paint.

The black paint fell on the ground.

When the rain stopped Brenda was black and grey again.

'Oh dear,' said Brenda. 'That wasn't a good idea.'

'I like you black and grey,' said James the elephant.

'I like you black and grey,' said Ryan the lion.

Even Kate the snake said, 'I like you black and grey.'

'I shall stay black and grey after all,' said Brenda.

And the rain stopped and the sun shone again."

"Thank you, Aunt Emily," said the children.

"That was a good story."

Aunt Emily smiled to herself.

"I shall stay black and grey too," she said.

Heavenly Father,
You have made us as we are.
Help us to be happy to be ourselves
and not be jealous of others.
Amen.

Chapter three

JAMES THE ELEPHANT

Aunt Emily was sitting in her chair.

It was a very hot day.

The children were playing in the sun.

The children ran to Aunt Emily.

"Tell us a story, please," they said.

"I will when you are sitting down," said Aunt Emily.

"I will tell you a story about an elephant.

The name of the elephant was James.

James lived in the jungle.

He lived with his mother and his father.

James was not always a good elephant.

James did not always go to school.

James could not read very well.

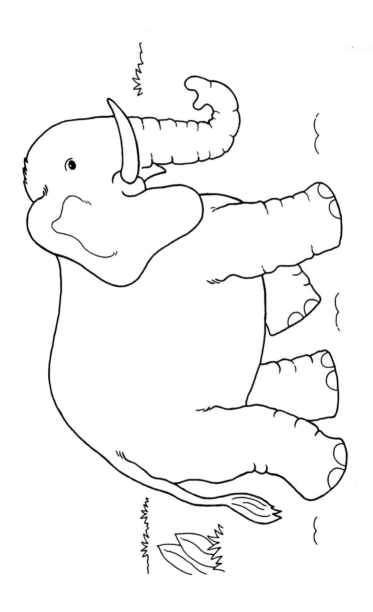

If James went to school he would learn to read.

His mother told James to go to school.

His father told James to go to school.

But James did not go.

He played in the jungle with his friends.

He played with Brenda the zebra.

He played with Ryan the lion.

He even played with Kate the snake.

They played hide-and-seek in the jungle.

It was hard for James to hide as he was very big.

James tried hard to hide.

But Brenda the zebra and Ryan the lion could see James.

Kate the snake was hard to find.

She hid in trees.

She hid in long grass.

She always won the game.

James got cross because he did not win.

He got cross because he was too big to hide.

He got cross because Kate the snake always won.

"One day," said Aunt Emily, "all the animals were in the jungle.

They were playing hide-and-seek again.

James the elephant, Ryan the lion and Brenda the zebra went to hide.

'I am going to win,' said James.

'Even Kate the snake will not find me.'

Brenda the zebra hid.

Ryan the lion hid.

James could not find anywhere to hide.

James ran through the jungle.

On a tree were some words.

The words were: 'Deep water ahead – take care!'

James did not go to school.

James could not read the words.

James ran on through the jungle.

The trees stopped.

The grass stopped.

The road stopped.

James did not stop.

There was a big splash.

There was a loud shout.

There was a very wet elephant.

James' mother came to see.

James' father came to see.

Ryan the lion and Brenda the zebra came to see.

Even Kate the snake came to see.

'You can't hide there!' said Kate the snake.

'Go to school, James, and learn to read,' said James' mother and father.

'Then you will not get so wet.'

The sun smiled on James and made him dry again.

The next day James went to school.

James could soon read very well."

"Thank you, Aunt Emily," said the children. "That was a good story."

Heavenly Father,
Thank you for my school.
Thank you for all the fun and friends I have there.
Thank you for all the things I can learn.
Help me to learn to read well.
Amen.

Chapter four

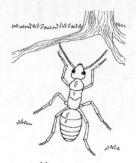

WILLIAM THE ANT

One day Aunt Emily was sweeping the floor.

Running over the floor was an ant.

Aunt Emily put down her brush and sat on her chair.

The children saw Aunt Emily and ran over to her.

"Tell us a story, please," they said.

"I will when you are sitting down," she said.

"I will tell you a story about an ant," she said.

"The name of the ant was William.

One day William was eating the root of a tree.

'I wish I was big like a tree,' said William,

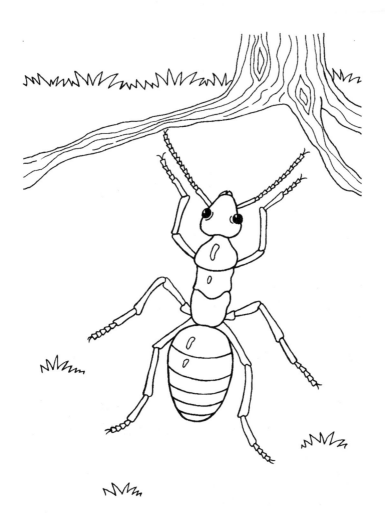

23

'and not small like an ant.'

As soon as William wished he was a tree he became a tree.

'It's fun being a tree,' said William.

He waved his branches about.

The day got older and the sun got hotter.

It was hot being a tree.

There is no shade when you are a tree.

The sun got hotter and hotter.

'I wish I was the sun,' said William.

As soon as William wished he was the sun he became the sun.

'It's fun being the sun,' said William.

He shone on Brenda the zebra.

He shone on James the elephant.

He shone on Ryan the lion.

And he even shone on Kate the snake.

Below William a cloud came along.

William looked down and could not see the animals.

Below him was this fluffy cloud.

The cloud stopped him shining on the animals.

'I wish I was a cloud,' said William.

As soon as William wished he was a cloud he became a cloud.

'It's fun being a cloud,' said William.
He made it rain on all the animals.
It rained on James the elephant.
It rained on Ryan the lion.
It rained on Brenda the zebra.
It even rained on Kate the snake.
Bang!
'Ouch!' said William.
William, the cloud, had bumped into a tall tree.
William rubbed his head where he had bumped it on the tree.
'I wish I was a tree again,' said William.
As soon as William wished he was a tree he became a tree again.
'It's fun being a tree,' said William.
He waved his branches about.

He waved at Brenda the zebra.
He waved at Ryan the lion.
He waved at James the elephant.
He even waved at Kate the snake.
Then he began to feel an itch.
It was an itch in his roots.
He couldn't scratch the itch.
He looked down.
An ant was eating his roots.
The ant was making him itch.
'I wish I was an ant,' said William.
As soon as William wished he was an ant he became an ant.
And the sun smiled at William who was in the shade of the tree."

"Thank you, Aunt Emily, that was a funny story," said the children.

Loving Father,
You have made me how I am.
Help me to be happy to be myself,
and help me to bring happiness to other people.
Amen.

Chapter five

DAWN THE FAWN

It was a very hot day.

Aunt Emily sat down in her chair.

The children saw Aunt Emily sit down.

They ran over to her.

"Tell us a story, please," they said.

"I will when you are sitting down," said Aunt Emily.

"I will tell you a story about a baby deer.

Her name was Dawn the fawn.

A fawn is a baby deer.

Dawn was not always a good fawn.

Dawn's mother told her to stay near her.

Her mother said, 'There is danger away from me.

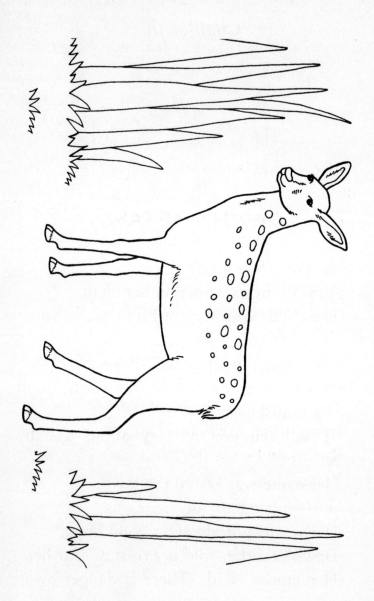

You must never run away to play on your own.'

But Dawn the fawn did not always do what her mother told her.

She liked to play on her own.

She liked to run away from her mother.

One day her mother went to sleep.

Dawn slowly tip-toed away from her mother.

Her mother did not wake up.

Dawn went into the jungle.

It was dark in the jungle.

Dawn could not see so well.

But she could hear well.

She heard a roar.

She jumped in the air when she heard the roar.

The roar was close by.

It was Ryan the lion who had roared.

Ryan saw Dawn the fawn.

Ryan knew Dawn should be with her mother.

Ryan spoke to Dawn.

'Dawn, you should be with your mother,' said Ryan.

'You are in danger in the jungle.

I have had my dinner and I am not a hungry lion.

But hungry lions eat fawns.

Go back to your mother.'

But Dawn did not go back to her mother.

Dawn went to the river to get a drink.

Dawn saw a big head, with small ears and lots of teeth, swimming in the river.

It was Jock the croc.

Jock knew that Dawn the fawn should be with her mother.

Jock the croc spoke to Dawn.

'Dawn, you should be with your mother.

You are in danger by the river.

I have had my dinner and I am not a hungry croc.

But hungry crocs eat fawns.

Go back to your mother.'

But Dawn did not go back to her mother.

Dawn went into the long grass.

Kate the snake was in the long grass.

Kate knew Dawn should be with her mother.

Kate spoke to Dawn.

'Dawn, your mother is looking for you.

Your mother does not know where you are.

You are in danger in the long grass.

Go back to your mother now!'

This time Dawn did go back to her mother.

'Dawn, you have not been a good fawn,' said her mother.

'You must stay with me and never run off on your own again.'

Dawn was a lucky fawn," said Aunt Emily.

"But don't you ever run away from your mothers."

"That was a good story," said the children.

And the sun smiled on Aunt Emily and the children.

Loving Father,
Sometimes we get lost and cannot see Mum or Dad –
But you can see us and you will look after us.
Thank you that you love us so much.
Amen.

Chapter six

SID THE KID

Aunt Emily had lost some buttons.

They were not on her table.

They were not in her cupboard.

They were not in her button bag.

She sat on her chair to think about them.

The children saw Aunt Emily and ran over to her.

"Tell us a story, please," they said.

"I will when you are sitting down," said Aunt Emily.

"I will tell you a story about a baby goat.

A baby goat is called a kid.

This story is about Sid the kid.

Sid was not always a very clever kid.

Sometimes Sid ate silly things.

Sid's mother told him to take care about what he ate.

One day Sid ran away from his mother and went off on his own.

There was no one to play with in the long grass.

There was no one to play with in the jungle.

Sid went to the village but there was no one to play with in the village.

Sid went down the road to the houses.

It was a hot day and the doors were open and Sid looked in the houses.

Some had children in them who called out to Sid.

Some had dogs in them who barked at Sid.

One house did not have any children or a dog.

Sid went into that house.

Sid looked for something to eat.

On the table were some shiny buttons that looked like sweets.

Sid did not know they were buttons.

There were red buttons and blue ones and green ones.

Sid ate one of the red buttons.

Then he ate one of the blue buttons and one of the green ones.

The buttons were rather hard and tasted funny.

Sid heard someone coming.

Sid ran out of the house.

He went back to his mother.

Sid told his mother he had tummy-ache.

'Where have you been, Sid?' she said.

Sid told his mother he had been to the village.

He told her he had been in a house.

'Did you eat something?' said his mother.

'I ate some very hard sweets,' said Sid.

Sid had a pain in his tummy for the rest of the day.

'I don't think they were sweets,' said his mother, 'I think they were buttons. You will be fine again soon, but you must be careful what you eat.'

"Don't eat buttons," Aunt Emily told the children, "or you too will have a tummy-ache!"

"Thank you, Aunt Emily," said the children, "that was a funny story."

"By the way, I think a goat must have eaten my buttons!" said Aunt Emily.

Loving Father,
We often do what we shouldn't do,
even though we know better.
Help us to listen to our parents
and then to do what they say.
Amen.

Chapter seven

JOCK THE CROC

Aunt Emily looked out of her window.

She saw the children playing.

One little boy was not playing.

The boy's name was Joshua.

Joshua was sitting on his own under a tree.

Joshua did not look happy.

He wanted to play with the other children.

Joshua did not have any friends.

Aunt Emily sat on her chair.

The children saw Aunt Emily and ran to her.

"Tell us a story, please," they said.

"I will when you are sitting down," said Aunt Emily.

"I will tell you a story about a crocodile.

The name of the crocodile was Jock.

He was called Jock the croc.

Jock lived on his own in a river.

The other animals did not play with Jock the croc.

'Don't go near Jock,' said Dawn the fawn's mother.

'Don't go near Jock the croc,' said Brenda the zebra's mother.

'Don't go near Jock the croc,' said everyone's mother.

So nobody went near Jock the croc.

He had no one to play with and no one to talk to.

Jock the croc was very lonely.

'One friend would be nice,' said Jock the croc to himself.

'I would be happy with one friend.

We could play and talk if I had just one friend.'

Jock the croc was a sad crocodile.

One day it was very hot.

The animals were getting hotter and hotter.

Dawn the fawn was hot and so were Brenda the zebra and Sid the kid.

Even Kate the snake was hot.

'Let's go to the river,' said Sid the kid, 'and have a drink.'

The animals went with Sid to the river.

The sun had dried the river and the river bank was very muddy.

'I shall sink in the mud,' said Brenda the zebra.

'So shall we,' said Dawn the fawn and Sid the kid.

Jock the croc heard the animals.

Jock swam up the river by the mud.

'Please don't run away,' said Jock the croc.

'I think I can help you get to the water.

I will lie in the mud and you can walk along my back.'

The animals did not know what to do.

Could they trust Jock?

Was it safe for them to walk along Jock's back?

The sun shone and it got hotter and hotter.

'I want a drink,' said Sid the kid, 'and I'm going to walk along Jock's back.'

Sid walked very slowly along Jock's back.

Jock was very still and did not move.

Sid had a good drink and came back to the river bank.

Dawn the fawn and Brenda the zebra had a good drink.

Even Kate the snake had a good drink.

'Thank you, Jock,' said all the animals.

'You have been a very good friend.

We shall come and see you again soon.'

'I shall not be lonely now,' said Jock the croc.

'Now I can play with the other animals and talk to them.'"

"Thank you, Aunt Emily," said the children.

"That was a good story."

The children ran away to play and Aunt Emily saw that Joshua was now playing with them.

Dear Jesus,
Thank you for being my best friend,
For loving me whatever I do,
For always being there with me.
Though I can't see you, help me to talk to you.
Amen.

Chapter eight

RITA THE CHEETAH

Aunt Emily was looking out of her window.

She saw the children playing.

They were having races.

One boy ran much faster than all the rest.

The name of the boy was Joseph.

"I'm the best runner," she heard Joseph say.

"I can run faster than all of you."

Aunt Emily sat on her chair.

The children saw Aunt Emily and ran over to her.

Joseph got there first.

"Tell us a story, please," they said.

"I will when you are sitting down," said Aunt Emily.

"I will tell you a story about a cheetah.

The name of the cheetah was Rita.

Cheetahs can run faster than any other animals.

One day Rita was playing with Ryan the lion, Brenda the zebra and Kate the snake.

'I can run faster than all of you,' said Rita the cheetah.

'I can run faster than Ryan or Brenda or Kate.'

'I don't think you can,' said Kate the snake. 'I think that sometimes I can run faster than you.'

'That's funny,' said Rita, 'a snake running faster than a cheetah! I can always run much faster than a snake!'

'We will have a race,' said Kate.

'I will start the race,' said Brenda the zebra.

'The race will be in the jungle,' said Kate.

'We will race when the sun gets up tomorrow morning.'

The next day Rita the cheetah and Kate the snake met Brenda and Ryan in the jungle.

It was a very thick jungle with big trees,

tall bushes and muddy water.

'We will race to the tallest tree in the jungle,' said Kate, 'and bring back a leaf from the tree.'

'I shall be there almost before you start,' said Rita.

'Ready, steady, go!' shouted Brenda.

Kate the snake slid up a tree and out along a branch.

Rita pushed her head into the bushes and tried to find the way.

Kate slid off one branch onto another, and then another.

Kate was getting near to the tallest tree in the jungle.

Rita did not know where she was.

One bush looked just like another one.

Rita fell into some muddy water.

Rita came out of a bush and saw Brenda the zebra and Ryan the lion.

Rita had got back to where she had started!

Kate slid down the tallest tree in the jungle.

Kate picked a leaf from the tree.

She took the leaf back to the other animals.

'Kate is the winner,' said Brenda, 'Kate was the fastest.'

'Well done, Kate, you won,' said Rita, with a smile.

'Now I will stop telling everyone I am the fastest animal.'"

"That was a good story," said the children.

"Yes," said Joseph, "that was a very good story."

Loving Father,
Thank you for all the things I can do well.
Help me not to boast about them.
Please help me to do better with the things I don't do well.
Amen.

Chapter nine

TIPPO THE HIPPO

"I don't think I will clean my house today," said Aunt Emily to herself.

"I will go and sit in my chair and think about it."

The children saw Aunt Emily and ran over to her.

"Tell us a story, please," they said.

"I will when you are sitting down," said Aunt Emily.

"I will tell you a story about a hippo.

The hippo's name was Tippo.

Tippo was a lazy hippo.

Tippo never did anything today that he could leave until tomorrow.

Tippo's mother and father did not know what to do about Tippo.

'Please Tippo,' said his mother, 'come and help us get some food.'

'I will soon,' said Tippo.

But Tippo just went back to sleep.

'Please Tippo,' said his father, 'come for a swim with me.'

'I will soon,' said Tippo.

But Tippo just went back to sleep.

'I don't know what we are going to do with Tippo,' said his mother.

'Nor do I,' said his father, 'he gets more lazy every day.

He just lies in the river doing nothing.'

The sun shone on the river.

It got hotter and hotter and hotter.

The river began to dry up.

'Tippo,' said his mother, 'you must come with us to find a new river.'

'I will soon,' said Tippo.

But Tippo just went back to sleep again.

The sun shone and the river dried up.

The river turned into thick, sticky mud.

In the middle of the mud was a hippo called Tippo!

Tippo woke up and saw the mud.

'Someone's stolen my river,' he said.

Tippo tried to get out of the mud.

He tried to lift his left leg but it was stuck.

He tried to lift his right leg but it was stuck.

Tippo's mother and father came to the river bank.

'You're a real stick-in-the-mud!' they said.

'Help!' said Tippo.

'We will soon,' said his mother and father.

'But I'm hungry,' said Tippo.

'You will soon be out of the mud,' said his mother.

'Look at the sky,' said his father.

The sun was hiding behind some clouds.

Soon some drops of rain began to fall.

Soon it began to rain hard.

It rained harder and harder and harder.

The river began to flow again.

The water got deeper and deeper and deeper.

The water flowed around Tippo.

Soon Tippo could swim again.

'I'm sorry I have been a lazy hippo,' he said.

'I don't want to be a stick-in-the-mud again! I will help you find some food and I will go for a swim with you.'"

"That was a funny story," said the children.

"Yes," said Aunt Emily to herself. "I think I will clean the house today after all."

Loving Father,
We miss so much when we are lazy.
Help us always to work and play as hard as we can.
Amen.

Chapter ten

MYRTLE THE TURTLE

Aunt Emily looked out of her window to see if the sun was shining.

The sun was hiding behind a big black cloud and was nowhere to be seen.

Not only was the sun hiding but it was raining hard.

"Oh dear," said Aunt Emily, "I wanted to get my washing dry."

And Aunt Emily sat down sulkily with her head in her hands.

The children saw Aunt Emily and ran over to her.

"Tell us a story, please," they said.

"I will when you are sitting down," said Aunt Emily.

"I will tell you a story about a turtle.

The turtle's name was Myrtle.

Myrtle was a turtle who used to sulk.

She sulked if she didn't get her own way.

She sulked if her mother told her off.

She sulked if someone else won a game.

Myrtle was a sulky turtle.

'You won't have any friends if you sulk,' said Myrtle's mother.

One day Kate the snake and Dawn the Fawn came to Myrtle's home.

'Will you come and play with us, Myrtle?' they asked.

'Yes,' said Myrtle, 'I will come and play with you.'

Kate the snake and Dawn the fawn and Myrtle the turtle played chase.

First Dawn was it and she chased Kate the snake and Myrtle the turtle.

Kate wriggled under a big stone and Dawn could not catch her.

Myrtle ran away as fast as her little legs would let her but Dawn soon caught her.

Myrtle was now chasing the others.

She chased Kate the snake but Kate always wriggled away from her.

She chased Dawn the fawn but Dawn always ran away from her.

Myrtle began to get hot and cross.

'It's not fair,' she said, 'you can both move quicker than me.'

Myrtle stopped in the middle of the path where they were playing.

Myrtle pulled her head into her shell and sat down and sulked.

Dawn the fawn and Kate the snake looked at Myrtle and quietly tiptoed away.

Ten minutes later Myrtle put her head out of her shell.

Myrtle looked around her but Dawn the fawn and Kate the snake had gone.

'Oh dear,' said Myrtle, 'I don't think they want to play with me any more.'

'Nobody likes sulky turtles,' said her mother later.

'Nobody will play with you if you sulk.'"

"Thank you, Aunt Emily," said the children.

"That was a good story."

Soon the sun was shining and Aunt Emily smiled to herself as she hung out her washing to dry.

Loving Father,
there are times when we are not very nice to be
with, times when we are sulky or we are cross.
Help us to remember all the good things we have
and to be happy.
Amen.

Chapter eleven

PRISCILLA THE GORILLA

Aunt Emily looked out of her window.

It was a lovely day and she went outside and sat down on her chair.

The children saw Aunt Emily sit down and they ran over to her.

"Tell us a story, please," they said.

"I will when you are sitting down," said Aunt Emily.

"I will tell you a story about a gorilla.

The gorilla's name was Priscilla.

Priscilla was not always a very clever gorilla.

Priscilla did not think that some of the other animals were nice to play with.

'No,' said Priscilla, when Sid the kid asked her to play.

'No – I do not play with goats. Gorillas would never play with animals that eat anything they find.'

'No,' said Priscilla, when Brenda the zebra asked her to play.

'No – I do not play with zebras. Gorillas would never play with animals that can't make up their minds whether they are wearing black or white.'

'No,' said Priscilla, when even Kate the snake asked her to play.

'No – gorillas never play with snakes. Gorillas would never play with animals that crawl about on their tummies.'

One day Priscilla was in the jungle.

She was swinging from tree to tree.

As she took hold of one branch it broke.

Priscilla fell through the other branches and landed with a bump on the ground.

When she tried to get up her leg hurt badly.

Priscilla could not move and it was getting dark.

'Help! Please help me someone,' she shouted.

Priscilla called out again and again.

At last she heard a noise.

Crawling along a branch was Kate the snake.

'Are you all right?' asked Kate the snake when she saw Priscilla.

'No,' said Priscilla, 'I have hurt my leg. Please get someone to help me.'

Kate crawled off at once.

Soon Brenda the zebra and Sid the kid came running through the jungle.

Sid helped Priscilla onto Brenda's back.

Brenda carried Priscilla through the jungle to her home.

When Priscilla's leg was better she went to see Brenda and Sid and even Kate the snake.

'Please may I play with you?' she asked.

'Yes, you can,' said the other animals, 'we are glad you want to be friends.'"

"Thank you, Aunt Emily," said the children.

"That was a good story."

Loving Father,
You love all people, whoever they are
and whatever they have done.
Help me to do the same.
Amen.